The Tiny Snowflake

Arthur Ginolfi

Illustrations by Louise Reinoehl Max

Tommy NELSON

www.tommynelson.com

A Division of Thomas Nelson, Inc.
www.ThomasNelson.com

Dedicated to my parents, Arthur and Marie Ginolfi;

my wife, Susan; my daughters, Sara and Caroline; and my son, Daniel

You Are All Very Special!

Published in Nashville, Tennessee, by Tommy Nelson®, a Division of Thomas Nelson, Inc.

Scripture quoted from the *International Children's Bible*®, *New Century Version*®, copyright © 1986, 1988, 1999 by Tommy Nelson®, a Division of Thomas Nelson, Inc., Nashville, Tennessee 37214. Used by permission.

Library of Congress Cataloging-in-Publication Data

Ginolfi, Arthur.
    The tiny snowflake / written by Arthur Ginolfi.
      p. cm.
    Summary: Lacy the snowflake discovers what makes her special in God's world.
    ISBN 1-4003-0205-6
    [1. Self-esteem—Fiction. 2. Christian life—Fiction. 3. Snowflakes—Fiction. 4. Snow—Fiction.] I. Title.
PZ7.G438945Tg 2003
[E]—dc21
                                       2003004643

Printed in the United States of America

03 04 05 06 WRZ 5 4 3 2 1

I praise you because you made me in an amazing and wonderful way.

~PSALM 139:14

One winter night, high above the earth, where storm clouds gather and cold winds blow, all of the little water droplets began to freeze and turn into snowflakes.

As the snowflakes fell from the clouds, they were amazed at how different they were from one another.

But Lacy, the tiny snowflake, didn't want to be different.

She was so tiny, the winter wind swirled her around while the other snowflakes, with their splendid shapes and pretty patterns, all floated down around her.

Lacy wanted to be like them.

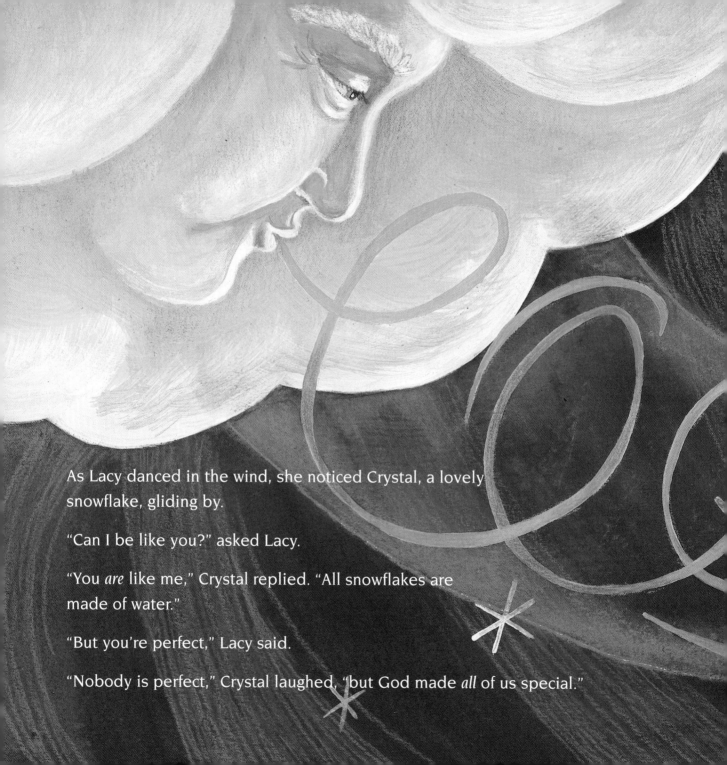

As Lacy danced in the wind, she noticed Crystal, a lovely
snowflake, gliding by.

"Can I be like you?" asked Lacy.

"You *are* like me," Crystal replied. "All snowflakes are
made of water."

"But you're perfect," Lacy said.

"Nobody is perfect," Crystal laughed, "but God made *all* of us special."

Lacy thought for a moment. "But how am I special?"

"Because you are you!" Crystal smiled.

"I don't understand," Lacy replied.

"You will," Crystal answered, gliding away.

How am I *special?* the tiny snowflake wondered, twirling in the wind.

Another snowflake tumbled down beside her. "How are *you* special?" Lacy asked.

"I am a fluffy snowflake, and I make the snow deep. That's how I'm special," he replied.

After the fluffy snowflake tumbled past, another
snowflake came spinning by.

"How are *you* special?" asked Lacy.

"I'm a slick snowflake, and I make the snow
slippery. That's how I'm special," he
answered and spun away.

Soon, another snowflake came spiraling by. "How are *you* special?" asked Lacy.

"I'm a delicate snowflake, and I make the snow soft. That's how I'm special," she said, spiraling away.

"But how am *I* special?" Lacy asked, looking into the cold, night sky.

Just before the sun began to rise, the winter wind howled one last time and blew all of the snowflakes down to the ground.

All of them, except Lacy.

The tiny snowflake took one last whirl in the wind and then slowly floated down, down, down, until she came to rest on top of the blanket of snow.

Everything was dark and quiet.

"Maybe," Lacy cried, "tiny snowflakes like me just aren't very special."

Then, as the bright, morning sun rose into the sky and peeked through the clouds, something wonderful happened—

Lacy began to sparkle!

As Lacy sparkled, the snow began to glisten!
She looked around and saw the hillside covered
in tiny sparkles reflecting the early morning
light. She was amazed at the beauty of it all.

At that moment, Lacy remembered Crystal's words, *God made all of us special.*

"That's it!" Lacy shouted. "I'm a sparkly snowflake, and I make the snow glisten!" She beamed with pride. "God *did* make all of us special! Even tiny snowflakes like me."

And Lacy, the tiny snowflake, was happy just being herself.